DATE DUE

0 1 APR 2009		

Author		
HANS C. ANDERSTIAN		

Title CHARLES PERRAULT
EMPEROR'S NEW CLOTHES
STEADFAST TIN SOLDIER
PUSS N BOOTS $7⁹⁹

Date	Name	Class
0 1 APR 2009	Core	

HANS C. ANDERSTIAN
PUSS N BOOTS
398   + 2 $7⁹⁹

The Emperor's New Clothes

The Steadfast Tin Soldier

Hans Christian Andersen

Puss in Boots

Charles Perrault

Illustrated by Michael Fiodorov

TREASURE TREE™

World Book, Inc.
a Scott Fetzer company
Chicago   London   Sydney   Toronto

Copyright © 1992
World Book, Inc.
525 West Monroe Street
Chicago, Illinois 60661

authorized English translation of *La Fiabe piu' Belle*,
© 1990 Happy Books s.r.l.
Illustrations © 1990 Happy Books s.r.l.

Printed in the United States of America
ISBN 0-7166-1629-7
Library of Congress Catalog Card No. 91 65768

Cover design by Rosa Cabrera

C/IC

The Emperor's New Clothes

A long, long time ago there lived an emperor who was so fond of elegant new clothes that he spent all his money on his wardrobe. He didn't care about his soldiers, or the theater, or rides in the woods, unless they gave him a chance to show off his new clothes. He had a different outfit for every hour of the day. With other rulers, it was often said, "He is in his council room." But this emperor spent so much time changing clothes that his subjects always said, "The emperor is in his dressing room!"

In the great city where the emperor kept his court, life was busy. Every day strangers arrived, and among them were some rogues. One day it became known that two master weavers had arrived. It was said that they were able to weave the most extraordinary cloth imaginable. Not only were its colors and designs of incomparable beauty, but the cloth also had a marvelous power: it was invisible to

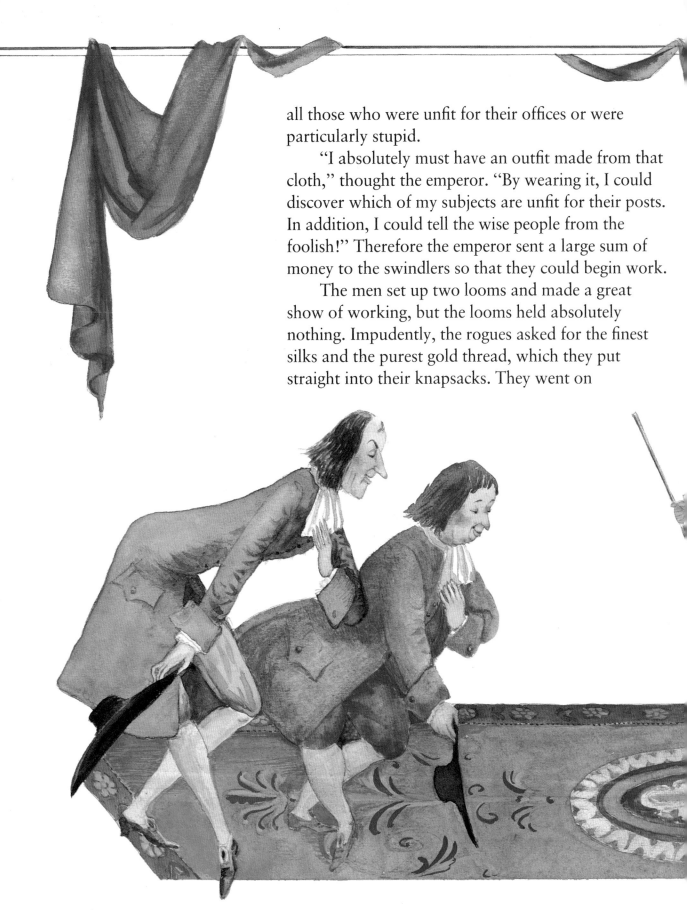

all those who were unfit for their offices or were particularly stupid.

"I absolutely must have an outfit made from that cloth," thought the emperor. "By wearing it, I could discover which of my subjects are unfit for their posts. In addition, I could tell the wise people from the foolish!" Therefore the emperor sent a large sum of money to the swindlers so that they could begin work.

The men set up two looms and made a great show of working, but the looms held absolutely nothing. Impudently, the rogues asked for the finest silks and the purest gold thread, which they put straight into their knapsacks. They went on pretending to work on the looms until late each night.

"I wonder how the weavers are getting on with my cloth," thought the emperor after a while. But then he remembered that stupid or incompetent people would not be able to see the cloth. That made him hesitate to make the inspection himself. He was sure he had nothing to fear. Nevertheless, he preferred to send someone else.

All the citizens had heard of the miraculous cloth and waited impatiently to find out just how stupid and incompetent their neighbors were.

"I will send my honest old minister to the weavers," the emperor decided at last. "He is the

person best qualified to judge the quality of the cloth. He is a man of good sense, and nobody is more fit for office than he."

So the faithful old minister went to the room where the two rogues were pretending to work at empty looms. "My word," he thought, staring hard, "I can see nothing at all!" But, naturally, he was careful not to say this aloud.

The impostors invited him to take a closer look. "Isn't the design perfect?" they asked. "Aren't the colors charming?" The poor old minister peered even more closely at the empty looms. Still, he could see nothing there, for the simple reason that there was nothing to see.

"Poor me!" thought the minister. "Is it possible that I am stupid? The idea never crossed my mind before, and it must not cross anyone else's mind now! Can it be that I am unfit for my office? No, that cannot be! I must never say that I cannot see the cloth!"

"You have not said if you like it . . ." said one of the rogues, still pretending to weave.

"Oh . . . yes, it's marvelous!" said the minister, putting on his spectacles. "What a design! What colors! Yes, I will be sure to tell the emperor I am immensely pleased."

"That is most kind of you!" replied the weavers. Then they began describing the colors and unusual quality of the cloth. The old minister listened carefully, so that he could repeat their exact words to the emperor. And that is just what he did.

Then the rogues asked for more supplies of money, of silk, and of gold thread, which they needed, they said, to continue their work. Instead, they put everything into their knapsacks. Not even a thread

reached the empty loom where they pretended to work.

After a while, the emperor sent another trusted official to judge how the work was going. He wanted to know whether the clothes would be ready soon. The same thing happened to the second official as to the first. He looked and looked but, since the looms were empty, could not see a thing.

"Beautiful, isn't it?" asked the rogues, showing him the cloth and explaining the marvelous design that wasn't there.

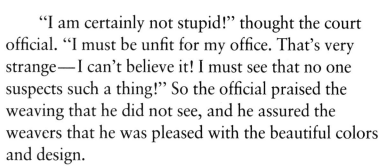

"I am certainly not stupid!" thought the court official. "I must be unfit for my office. That's very strange—I can't believe it! I must see that no one suspects such a thing!" So the official praised the weaving that he did not see, and he assured the weavers that he was pleased with the beautiful colors and design.

"Indeed, Your Majesty," he told the emperor, "it is the most beautiful cloth I ever saw!"

By now, the splendid cloth was the talk of the town. So the emperor decided to see it while it was still on the loom. Accompanied by a crowd of courtiers, including the two officials who had already been there, he went to visit the swindlers. They were

busily weaving with great energy, but without warp or woof.

"Isn't it magnificent?" asked the two old officials. "Observe, Your Majesty. What a design! What colors!" And they pointed to the empty loom, convinced that everyone else could see the cloth.

"What is going on here?" thought the emperor. "I can't see anything. This is terrible! Am I stupid? Am I unfit to be emperor? That would be intolerable." Aloud, he said, "Oh, how beautiful! I approve of it entirely."

The emperor smiled with satisfaction at the empty loom, for nothing in the world would make him admit that he saw nothing.

All the courtiers looked and looked again, but not one of them could see a thing. Nevertheless, they all repeated in chorus with the emperor, "How marvelous! How marvelous!" And they advised the emperor to have a complete outfit made, to wear in the great procession that was coming soon.

"That cloth is excellent!" they said to each other. "Superb!" And they all seemed genuinely impressed. So the emperor conferred a knighthood on each of the rogues, giving them the title of Knights of the Loom.

The night before the big procession, the two swindlers worked until dawn. They set sixteen candles burning in the window, so everyone could see how hard they were working. They pretended to lift the cloth from the loom. With large scissors they cut ample pieces of . . . air. They sewed with empty needles. And, at last, they cried, "Look! The emperor's robes are complete!"

Accompanied by his most important courtiers, the emperor went to be fitted. The two impostors raised their arms as if holding up something and said, "Here are the breeches and tights, this is the jacket, here is the mantle," and so on.

"The whole outfit is as light as a cobweb, Your Majesty," they exclaimed. "You will feel as if you were wearing nothing at all."

"Oh, yes!" breathed the courtiers, though none of them could see a thing. After all, there was nothing to be seen!

"And now, if Your Majesty would be gracious enough to undress?" asked the swindlers. "We shall be pleased to fit you with your new robes here in front of this mirror."

So the emperor took off his clothes, and the rogues pretended to dress him, garment by garment.

Finally, they pretended to tie a belt around his waist. Then they stood back while the emperor turned from side to side in front of the mirror.

"How regal you look, Your Majesty!" cried the courtiers. "What a wonderful fit! The style and colors are a marvel! A truly precious cloth!"

Then the master of ceremonies arrived. "The canopy to be held over Your Majesty has arrived," he said. "It is waiting in the square."

"Very well," said the emperor. "I am ready. My

new clothes fit well, don't they?" And he pretended to check the mirror one more time.

The lords-in-waiting fumbled about on the ground, pretending to pick up the train they couldn't see. Then they lined up behind the emperor with their hands raised, being careful not to let anyone know that they saw nothing.

Then the emperor began his march, walking beneath his rich canopy. The crowd in the streets and at the windows remarked, "Goodness! Look at the

emperor's new clothes. No one has ever seen the like. Look at the marvelous train. What a perfect fit!" No one wanted anyone else to think that he or she couldn't see the clothes, for fear of being thought stupid. Never had a royal outfit met with such success.

"But he hasn't got any clothes on!" said a little child.

"Listen to the voice of innocence!" exclaimed the child's father.

And everyone began to repeat the child's words.

"He has no clothes on! A child said it. The emperor isn't wearing any clothes!"

Very soon the whole crowd was shouting, "The emperor isn't wearing any clothes!" And the emperor realized that the crowd was right. But he thought to himself, "I must carry on to the end, or the parade will be ruined." So he drew himself up more proudly than before, while the lords-in-waiting followed, carrying a train that wasn't there.

The Steadfast Tin Soldier

Once there were twenty-five tin soldiers. They were all brothers, made from the same old tin spoon. They carried muskets in their arms and stood at attention with heads held high. Their uniforms were of blue, white and red, very fine indeed. The first words they heard in this world, when the lid was removed from their box, were "Tin soldiers!" A little boy shouted the words and clapped his hands in delight. The soldiers were a present for his birthday, and now he lined them up on the table.

All the soldiers were exactly the same, except for one. He had only one leg because he had been made last, when there was not quite enough tin left. Yet he stood as firmly on one leg as the others did on two. And it is of him that our story tells.

On the table with the soldiers were many other toys, but the one you noticed first was a castle of painted cardboard. You could look through its tiny windows right into the rooms. In front, tiny trees surrounded a little mirror that stood for a lake. Little wax swans swam there, gazing at their own reflections. And prettiest of all was a little lady who stood in the open doorway of the castle.

She, too, was cardboard but wore a dress of the finest silk. A pale blue ribbon was draped about her shoulder and held by a sequin, a glittering jewel as big as her face. The lady held out both her arms in a graceful pose, for she was a ballerina. She kept one leg raised so high that the soldier could not see it. So he thought she had only one leg, like him.

"She would be the perfect wife for me!" he thought. "But she must be a lady of high rank. She lives in a castle, and I live in a box with twenty-four other soldiers. That's no place for her! Still, I would like to meet her." Then he positioned himself behind a snuff box on the table. From there he could gaze at the beautiful lady who stood on one leg without losing her balance.

That night all the other tin soldiers were put back in the box, and the people of the house went to bed. Then the toys began to play. They played house, and had battles, and held a ball. The tin soldiers rattled in their box because they wanted to play, but they could not get the lid off their box.

The nutcrackers turned somersaults, and the chalk danced noisily on the chalkboard. There was such a racket that the canary woke up and began to sing—in verse! The only ones who didn't move were the tin soldier and the little ballerina. She kept standing on tiptoe, with her arms outstretched. He, no less firm, stood upright on his one leg. His eyes never left her for a moment.

16

Then the clock struck twelve and—*pop!*—the lid of the snuff box flew open— the box was really a jack-in-the-box. Out jumped a little black goblin.

"Tin soldier!" cried the goblin, "Please keep your eyes to yourself!"

The tin soldier pretended not to hear.

"Just wait until tomorrow, then!" threatened the little goblin.

When tomorrow came, the little children got up, and they moved the tin soldier to the window ledge.

All of a sudden—whether the goblin or the wind caused it—the window flew open, and the tin soldier fell out, head first, from the third floor! He fell at a frightening speed, with his leg pointing up in the air. He landed on his head, his bayonet stuck between two cobblestones.

The maid and the little boy ran downstairs to look for him. Though they nearly stepped on him, they didn't see him. If only he would have called out, "Here I am!" they would have found him easily. But the tin soldier didn't think it was proper to cry out while in uniform.

It began to rain, one drop after another, until it was a perfect downpour. When it stopped, two boys came by. "Look at that!" said one of them. "It's a tin soldier! Let's send him on a fine trip!"

The boys made a boat out of newspaper and put the little tin soldier on board. Away he sailed, down the gutter, while the boys ran along, clapping their hands. Good heavens! What waves there were in the gutter, and what a strong current there was! Truly, it was a flood! The paper boat whirled around so fast that the tin soldier felt completely dizzy. Still, he remained steadfast, keeping his musket on his shoulder and looking straight ahead.

Suddenly the boat slipped into a long underground canal. It was completely dark there.

"Where on earth am I going?" thought the soldier. "I am sure this is all the fault of that goblin! If only the ballerina were here with me now, I wouldn't care if it were twice as dark!"

Just then, a great big water rat leaped out of the gutter. "Where is your passport?" he screeched. "To travel here, you must have a passport!"

But the tin soldier didn't say a word. He just held his musket more tightly than ever.

The boat sailed on, and the rat chased after it. Oh, how it gnashed its teeth! It cried out to all the sticks and straws, "Stop him! Stop him! He hasn't paid the toll! He hasn't even shown his passport!"

Meanwhile, the current was growing stronger and stronger, and at last the tin soldier saw a glimmer of daylight ahead. But he also began to hear a roar that would make the bravest person tremble. At the end of the tunnel, the water fell a long way down to a great canal. For the tin soldier, this danger was as great as it would be for us to go over a waterfall. But he was already so close that he couldn't stop. When the boat plunged over the edge, the poor soldier held himself as stiff as possible. No one could say that he showed any sign of fear.

The boat spun around three—no, four—times, and filled with water until it could do nothing but sink. The tin soldier stayed upright as the water reached his neck, the wet paper began to tear, and the water went over his head. Then the tin soldier thought of the graceful little ballerina he would never see again, and he said to himself:

> *Onward, onward, soldier brave,*
> *Each of us must face the grave!*

The paper boat fell apart, and the tin soldier sank down . . . and was instantly swallowed up by a large fish! How dark it was inside the fish. It was even darker than the tunnel, and much more cramped! But the tin soldier was not discouraged. He lay as straight as ever, his musket on his shoulder.

After a time, the fish began to twist and thrash about in a terrifying way, but at last it lay still. There came a flash of light. Daylight blazed, and someone cried, "The tin soldier!"

The fish had been caught, taken to market, and sold. In the kitchen, the cook had cut it open. Now she picked up the soldier with two fingers and carried him into the living room. There everyone wished to see the hero who had traveled in the belly of a fish. But the tin soldier was not boastful.

They set him on the table, and . . . what a strange world it is! The tin soldier found himself in the room he had left before. He saw the same children

and the same toys. There were the castle and the graceful little ballerina who still stood on one leg. She had been steadfast, too!

The tin soldier was so touched he would have cried, only he thought it was not fitting for a soldier to weep. He looked at the dancer and she looked at him, but neither one spoke a word.

Suddenly one of the children grabbed the tin soldier and threw him into the stove. The child had no reason for doing it, so it must have been the work of the goblin.

The tin soldier found himself in a great light and felt a suffocating heat, but he did not know whether the cause was the heat of the fire or of his warm love. He had lost his colors—whether from his travels or from grief he could not tell.

For the last time, he looked at the ballerina and she looked at him. He felt himself melting, yet he still stood straight, his musket on his shoulder.

Then a door opened and a gust of wind caught the ballerina. She flew like a sylph into the fire, to join the soldier. She flared up in flame and was gone. Then the tin soldier melted away.

The next day, when the maid cleaned out the grate, she found what remained of the tin soldier: a little tin heart. Nothing remained of the dancer but her sequin, and that was burned as black as coal. The heart and the sequin lay as close as the love between the tin soldier and the little ballerina.

Puss in Boots

There once was an old miller who, when he died, left his mill, his donkey, and his cat to his three sons. The sons easily divided these things among themselves. The eldest son received the mill, the second got the donkey, and the youngest was left with the cat. The poor lad was most upset at receiving such a poor inheritance. He said to himself, "If my two brothers work together, they can make an honest living. As for me, what good is a cat? I'll soon die of hunger!"

The cat heard all this but pretended not to. He said with a serious manner, "Do not fear, master. Just give me a sack and a pair of hunting boots, and I'll show you that you haven't done so badly!"

Although the cat's new owner was not convinced, he remembered seeing the animal using some clever tricks to catch rats and mice. For instance, he hung from the rafters by his feet, or hid in the flour, pretending to be dead. So the lad thought that maybe

the cat could help him out of his misery. When the cat had what he had asked for, he put on the boots and flung the sack over his shoulder. Then he set off toward an area where there were large numbers of rabbits. The cat put some ears of wheat and some lettuce leaves into the sack. After that, he lay down and pretended to be dead. He was waiting for some poor rabbit, unused to the wicked ways of the world, to hop into the bag for the food that was inside.

In no time, the cat had his first success. An inexperienced little rabbit hopped into the sack and the cunning cat immediately pulled the string, trapping the rabbit. Pleased with his hunting skills, the cat went straight to the palace and asked to speak to the king. He was taken into the royal apartment. There, with a deep bow, the cat said, "Sire, I bring you a wild rabbit. My lord, the Marquis of Carabas (a made-up name—the first one that came to the cat's mind) commanded me to bring it to you as a gift."

"Tell your master," the king replied, "that I thank him and appreciate his kindness."

Another time, the cat hid in the wheat field, taking his sack with him again. When two partridges entered, he pulled the string and caught them both. Then he took them to the king just as he had done with the rabbit. The king happily accepted the two partridges and offered the cat some milk in return.

The cat continued to bring to the king gifts of game from his master, the Marquis of Carabas. One day, the cat learned that the king planned to go for a ride along the riverbank with his daughter, the most beautiful princess imaginable. He told his master, "If you follow my advice, your fortune will soon be made. Just take a bath in the river at a place I will show you. Then leave the rest to me."

"The Marquis of Carabas" did what his cat advised him, though he had no idea what good it would do him. While the marquis was bathing, the king passed by. The cat began to shout at the top of his voice, "Help, help, the Marquis of Carabas is drowning!"

Hearing these cries, the king put his head out of his carriage window. He recognized the cat who had brought him so many gifts of game and ordered his guards to go to the aid of the Marquis of Carabas. As they were dragging the poor marquis from the river, the cat approached the carriage. He told the king that while his master had been in the water, thieves had

come and stolen away his clothes. (The cat had actually hidden them beneath a big rock.)

The king immediately sent one of his officers back to the palace to fetch some of his finest clothes for the Marquis of Carabas.

The king treated the young man very kindly. And, because he looked so good in the fine clothes— for he was a handsome, well-built young man—the king's daughter liked him as well. After just two or three respectful but tender glances from the Marquis of Carabas, the princess fell hopelessly in love with him! The king insisted that the young man join them in their carriage and enjoy the outing with them.

Seeing that his plan was working, the cat ran on ahead. He came across some peasants cutting hay in a field. He said to them, "Good people, you must tell the king that these fields belong to the Marquis of Carabas. If you don't, you will be cut to pieces like sliced ham!" Soon the king passed by and asked them whose fields they were working. The cat's threat had frightened them, so they replied together, "They belong to the Marquis of Carabas."

"You have some fine land," the king said to the Marquis of Carabas.

"As you can see," replied the marquis, "these fields provide a good crop each year."

The cunning cat ran on farther ahead and met with some workers stacking freshly cut wheat. "Good harvesters," he said, "you must tell the king that all this wheat belongs to the Marquis of Carabas. If you don't, you will be chopped into mincemeat!"

The king, who passed a minute later, asked to whom the crops belonged. The peasants replied, "The Marquis of Carabas." The king commended the marquis on his fertile land.

The cat continued to run ahead of the carriage, saying the same thing to everybody he met. The king was amazed at the vast possessions of the Marquis of Carabas.

The cat finally came to a beautiful castle that belonged to the richest ogre there ever was. All the land the king had passed through belonged to the ogre's castle. The cat had taken care to find out who this ogre was and to know what he did. Now he asked to speak with the ogre, saying that it would be rude to pass by his castle without dropping in to pay his respects. The ogre received him with as much kindness as might be expected from an ogre.

"I have been told," said the cat, "that you have the ability to change into any kind of animal—even a lion or an elephant."

"It's true," replied the ogre harshly. "And to prove it, I will change into a lion."

The cat was so frightened to find himself face to face with a lion that he scuttled up onto the roof. This gave him some difficulty, for his tall boots were not suitable for going out onto roof tiles.

After a bit, when the ogre had changed back into his usual shape, the cat came back down. He admitted being very afraid. "I have also been assured," he went on, "that you can also change yourself into a very small animal, like a mouse or a rat. I must confess I find that impossible to believe."

"Impossible?" bellowed the ogre. "Watch this!" He immediately changed into a mouse that began running about on the floor. As soon as the cat saw this, he leaped upon him and gobbled him up!

Meanwhile the king saw, in passing, the castle of the ogre, and he wanted to go inside. Hearing the sound of the carriage on the drawbridge, the cat rushed out and said, "Your majesty, welcome to the castle of the Marquis of Carabas."

"Why, sir!" exclaimed the king. "This castle is yours as well? I have never seen anything as beautiful as this courtyard, with these buildings around it. May we go inside?"

The marquis gave his arm to the young princess and they followed the king into a huge hall. There they found a banquet laid out. The ogre had prepared it for some friends he had been expecting that day. The friends, however, didn't dare enter when they

learned the king was there. The king was as enchanted by the excellent qualities of the Marquis of Carabas as was his daughter, who was obviously head over heels in love.

After considering the vast wealth the marquis seemed to possess, the king turned to the young man and said, "Well, sir, it is up to you if you wish to become my son-in-law!"

Bowing deeply, the marquis accepted the honor, and he and the princess were wedded that very day. The cat became a great lord and never again ran after mice—except for fun.

To Parents

Children delight in hearing and reading fairy tales. "The
Emperor's New Clothes," "The Steadfast Tin Soldier," and "Puss
in Boots" will provide your child with entertaining stories as well
as a bridge into learning some important concepts. Here are a few
easy and natural ways your child can express feelings and
understandings about the stories. You know your child and can
best judge which ideas he or she will enjoy most.

Most classic fairy tales were originally
passed down from one generation to the
next through the art of storytelling.
Andersen wrote his tales so that they would
sound best when read aloud. Encourage
your child to learn his or her favorite story
well enough to tell it to someone.

Oftentimes, storybook characters have to
learn something. Talk with your child about
what the characters in these tales had to learn.

Go to a library with your child and borrow
other versions of the fairy tales in this book.
After sharing them, talk about how they are
similar to and different from the versions
in this collection. Encourage your child
to tell why one version is more appealing
than another.

Invite your child to rewrite one of the fairy
tales in a modern-day setting. Before your

child begins, talk about which parts of the
story might stay the same and which might
change. Encourage your child to illustrate
the new tale.

Ask your child which fairy-tale character in
this book would be fun to meet. Then pre-
tend to be that character and encourage
your child to ask you questions. Switch roles
so that your child becomes a character you'd
like to meet.

Libraries, schools, bookstores, and theaters
often host storytellers' performances of fairy
tales. Look in your newspaper to find out
where and when these events take place.
Look to see if plays or puppet shows of fairy
tales are being performed anywhere. From
a library, check out records and tapes of
fairy tales so that your child can hear how
different people tell them.